W9-CPZ-461

ABOUT THE BOOK

The big red barn that stood near the house made the young boy feel secure. It was where he had gone to cry when his mother died and later when his dad brought home a new mother. It was where he and his sister played in the hayloft and where the farm animals slept and ate and made their friendly, familiar sounds. But one night the smell of smoke awoke them, and the beloved red barn burned to the ground. Like the new mother, the new barn was another difficult change. With Grandpa's help they learn to adjust to the new, while keeping the old alive in their hearts, in this sensitive, touching companion piece to *Winter's Coming*.

A Let Me Read Book

THE BIG
RED BARN
by Eve Bunting
pictures by Howard Knotts

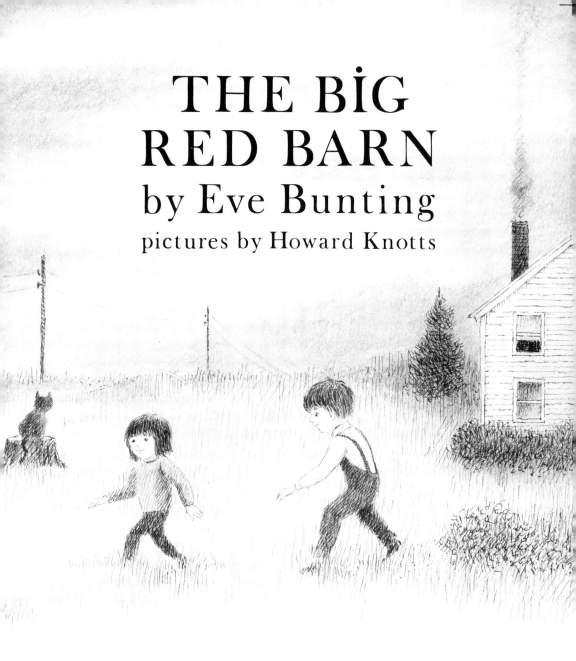

Harcourt Brace Jovanovich

New York and London

Text copyright © 1979 by Eve Bunting
Illustrations copyright © 1979 by Howard Knotts

All rights reserved. No part of this publication
may be reproduced or transmitted in any form or
by any means, electronic or mechanical, including
photocopy, recording, or any information storage
and retrieval system, without permission in
writing from the publisher.

Requests for permission to make copies of any part
of the work should be mailed to:
Permissions, Harcourt Brace Jovanovich, Inc.,
757 Third Avenue, New York, New York 10017

Printed in the United States of America

Library of Congress Cataloging in Publication Data
Bunting, Anne Eve.
The big red barn.
(A Let me read book)
SUMMARY: A youngster's sense of security is
threatened by the arrival of a stepmother and the
destruction of the old red barn on her family's farm.
[1. Barns—Fiction. 2. Stepmothers—Fiction.
3. Farm life—Fiction]. I. Knotts, Howard. II. Title.
PZ7.B91527Bm   [Fic]   78–12186
ISBN 0-15-207145-8
ISBN 0-15-611938-2 pbk.

First edition

B C D E

To my friends at Upper Iowa University—
thanks for sharing your red barns

Our big red barn sat across the yard from our house. It was ten times bigger than our house, though. Dad said that was because the barn sheltered more creatures.

Our cows and our fat pigs wandered in and out

of the barn all day long.

Susie's pet goat, Gertrude, had her own stall. Susie taught Gertrude a bunch of tricks. She bows when Susie snaps her fingers, but she won't bow for anyone else.

The hens roosted in the rafters at night.
Abraham, our rooster, took the highest rafter. As
soon as the sun set, we saw them there, the hens
fluffing their feathers like covers around their
heads.

A barn owl lived in the barn's darkest corner.
All we ever saw were his big yellow eyes. Once
we heard the quick swoop of his wings and felt
the air move. There was a tiny, small mouse cry.

8

Susie and I don't like the owl. We found a little mound of white bones in the owl's corner. They crumbled when we touched them. Grandpa says the owl does what he has to do, but Susie and I still don't like him.

We had a nest of kangaroo mice in our barn.

Susie took Emma down to see them. Emma's our new mom now that Dad's married to her. I didn't want Susie to show Emma our mice, but she did anyway.

The mice lived in the corner farthest from the owl. Susie and I hoped he would never find them. It was lucky the barn was so big. But that old owl's eyes were big too.

The hayloft was up above. When you bounced on a bale, hay dust danced in the air. The loft was warm and sneezy, and it smelled of summer.

When you looked down, you could see how the night barn looked to Abraham when he was high on his perch.

The hayloft was where I went when I needed to cry. It was very secret. That was where I went when Mom died. And that was where I went the day Dad brought Emma home.

Once I asked Dad why we always painted the barn red.

"Because it was red to begin with, when we bought the farm," he said.

"I expect red barn paint's the cheapest kind," Emma said.

"Red's the color barns are," Grandma said.

But it was Grandpa who made the most sense. "Red's the easiest color to see," he said. "It's comforting to look across the fields and say, 'There

she is. There's our big red barn. There's home.' "
Grandpa always says the best things.

We could see our barn most every place we
went. It was red against the green of grass, or the
brown of new-plowed fields, or the white of snow.

"There she is," I'd say. "There's our big red
barn. There's home." Of course, I didn't say it out
loud.

Then one night, right in the middle of the night, our big red barn caught fire.

It was Grandpa who smelled the smoke. Grandpa doesn't sleep much anymore. He banged on our doors and yelled, "Fire! Fire in the barn!"

We all woke up pretty quick.

Emma called the fire department while the rest of us ran for the barn.

"Gertrude, Gertrude," Susie cried, sobbing.

14

The hayloft was ablaze. Smoke oozed and billowed from the ventilators.

We got Gertrude out, and the cows and pigs. The hens and Abraham fluttered wildly past us.

Susie ran back in to save the kangaroo mice, but the nest was empty. We never saw the owl.

Dad and Emma had the big hose going. We carried water buckets from the house. But the fire was winning.

"Where's the darned fire engine?" Grandma
kept shouting.

"It's too late anyway," Dad said. "Once a barn
fire starts, it's too late."

We heard a slipping sort of crash inside.

"The loft's gone," Grandpa said.

16

The heat was so bad now that we had to stand very far back. I thought about the loft and how it was gone and the way it had smelled, and I began to cry. I realized that I had no place to go now when I needed to cry, and I remembered how I had cried when Mom died. And I cried even harder.

Then Susie started.

"Shut up," I said. "Why do you always have to do what I do?"

And that was when we heard the fire engines.

"A lot of use when it's all over," Grandma said.

But the firemen stretched their big fat hoses so they reached all the way to the river, and they sucked up the river water and poured it over everything they could reach.

"I'm sorry about your barn, Craig," Emma said
to Dad, and Dad put his arm around her
shoulders.

I walked away.

Susie and I leaned out of our bedroom window for the longest time that night.

The barn was burned all the way to the ground. Everything was a mess of mud and water, and there was a terrible smell of smoke.

The cows and the pigs and the hens and Gertrude were in the yard, mooing and grunting and baaing and clucking and looking sorry for themselves.

"Will Dad build another barn?" Susie asked.

"He has to," I said.

"It won't be the same," Susie said.

I knew that.

Three days later the bulldozers came, and when they'd gone, there was no trace of the old barn.

The new one came in big pieces.

"Prefabricated aluminum," Dad said. "Wood's not cheap anymore."

"What's prefabricated mean?" I asked.

"It means big pieces made to fit together, like a giant jigsaw puzzle," said Dad.

The new barn would be as big as the old one and shaped the same.

"I thought we'd like that best," Dad said.

I didn't like it at all.

Dad bought hay from John Culbertson on the next farm.

"You ever find what started the fire?" Mr. Culbertson asked.

"They figure a rat gnawed through some wiring," Dad said.

I thought about that a lot. A rat's little teeth, chewing, chewing . . . and our big red barn was gone forever.

The new barn was finished. It shone silver in
the sun.

Susie got to lead Gertrude in first. Then we
shooed the cows and the pigs in to let them see
it. They weren't a bit happy. The hens and
Abraham skittered about the yard and wouldn't be
shooed anywhere.

24

"Let them be," Emma said. "Change is hard. They'll take to it in time."

"You're wrong," I thought.

"It's so clean," Susie complained.

"It smells like a tin box," I said.

I ran down to the river, where the beaver had
dammed it up. I wished I could go to the old
hayloft because that's the way I felt, but the old
hayloft was gone.

I lay in the grass for a while, and then I sat up

and watched Emma hanging clothes on the clothesline. Susie was helping her. Once Emma bent down and smoothed back Susie's hair. They were far enough away so that if I squinched my eyes, I could pretend Emma was Mom.

I heard Grandpa's whistle, and I answered it. He sat in the grass beside me and began skimming stones.

"You think we should paint the new barn?" he asked.

"Red paint won't make it be the old barn," I said.

"No," Grandpa said. "What's gone's gone. We have to let go of it."

"The new barn's not going to take the old barn's place." I sounded fierce and I felt fierce. Inside me things seemed to be boiling over.

"That's right," Grandpa said. "The new barn has to make its own place. It will if we give it a chance." He sat very still, and I couldn't tell when he looked across the field if he was looking at the barn or at Emma. Grandpa always knew how I felt.

"It's not wrong to forget?" I asked.

"Who said anything about forget," Grandpa said. "We won't ever forget."

For some reason the boiling inside me seemed
to ease and slow. I shaded my eyes and looked at
the sun shimmer on the barn and I wanted to like
it. It was part of our family now . . . part of us.
Inside it the pigs and the cows and Gertrude were

doing their best to make it smell the way the old
barn smelled. The kangaroo mice might come
back. And the old owl.

"I expect silver's the next best color for a barn
after red," I told Grandpa.

"I expect so," Grandpa said.

Eve Bunting was born and educated in Ireland and came to the United States in 1959 with her husband and three children. She is the author of many children's books, including *Winter's Coming,* and her stories have appeared in *Cricket* and *Jack and Jill.* Ms. Bunting resides in Pasadena, California.

Howard Knotts is a well-known artist, as well as a children's book illustrator, and his paintings have been widely exhibited. He collaborated with Eve Bunting on *Winter's Coming* and has written and illustrated *The Lost Christmas.* Mr. Knotts lives in a two-hundred-year-old house in Bangall, New York, with his wife, author-illustrator Ilse-Margret Vogel, and their nine cats.